GAY UNIVERSITY ROMANCE SHORT STORY COLLECTION

CONNOR WHITELEY

No part of this book may be reproduced in any form or by any electronic or mechanical means. Including information storage, and retrieval systems, without written permission from the author except for the use of brief quotations in a book review.

This book is NOT legal, professional, medical, financial or any type of official advice.

Any questions about the book, rights licensing, or to contact the author, please email connorwhiteley@connorwhiteley.net

Copyright © 2023 CONNOR WHITELEY

All rights reserved.

DEDICATION
Thank you to all my readers without you I couldn't do what I love.

DOUBTING IN LOVE

Tony Marks hadn't actually known he was gay before last Christmas at that amazing university psychology social with great music, great food and a really cute boy. Tony felt so strange because he was so drawn to that particular boy, never got his name but Tony would always remember him.

So as the party continued, Tony kept feeling more and more drawn to this amazing boy and just as the Christmas crowd started to go home. Tony found himself kissing his mystery boy, and considering how amazing he felt he was fairly sure he was gay.

And it just felt so right to him.

As Tony stood next to a small metal table with tea, coffee and those horrible polyester cups that smelt the coffee taste so fake, awful and just unreal. Tony made sure he held the table firmly, so firmly he felt his knuckles turn bright white.

The drinks next to him made, the large university meet room with its tables and chairs scattered around the room and its smooth white walls, fill up with hints of burnt coffee, disgusting herbal tea and some other strange smell that Tony didn't know.

He wanted to walk away from the table but he just felt so nervous.

Tony had been back to university for a few weeks now after the Christmas break and talking to his parents about… his new preference (that's what everyone wanted to call it and Tony was just going to let them), and they just said him as long as you're happy.

Even now Tony wasn't exactly sure what that meant. He knew deep down his parents loved him very much, but maybe they were still getting over the shock of finding out he was interested in men, since they refused to call him *outright gay*.

Tony had just laughed and even now he wasn't exactly sure what the hell had meant. He liked men and even since that Christmas Party he hadn't looked at a woman in the same way.

Then Tony supposed that he never really did in the first place. Sure he had had a few girlfriends because that's what the cool kids did, and your own self-worth was measured back in secondary school by how many female conquests you had, but Tony had never done that.

When all his sporty friends (who were admittingly rather hot retrospectively) had boasted about their latest girlfriends, Tony would just sit there and nod along. And if someone asked him about his own relationships, he would just lie.

So maybe that hot Christmas party had just helped him along and realise what had been missing in his life.

A man had been missing from it.

Tony just smiled to himself and just realising that felt amazing, and like it was just a part of who he was. Granted Tony was never ever going to tell his parents that, not until they were ready to hear such news.

And Tony was very willing to wait until then.

But as people started to come into the meeting room in all their different heights, looks and physiques, Tony just felt his stomach tighten.

He had never been to a gay meet up or event before, he didn't know what to expect. He didn't know if all these people wanted to chat, make new friends or just have sex. That was the problem with the gay community being so separate from the mainstream, all Tony had to go on was myths, fears and misconceptions.

That and he supposed he was just a bit concerned or embarrassed to be here in the first place. It wasn't like his parents would exactly be thrilled if they knew he was here mixing with *his kind*.

Then Tony saw some different gay men walk in as they laughed, joked and seemed like they were perfectly nice people, and Tony decided (or maybe it was more instinct) that he needed to stop thinking about others, and just focus on himself.

He wasn't here to impress anyone. He was here

to explore this new part of himself that felt so right, and if nothing worked out here then that was okay. He had tried and that was all that mattered.

But ideally Tony would meet some amazing guys, make a few new friends and in the best world possible, met a really cute man and… get to know him better.

Tony really wanted that to happen.

He just wanted to experience himself a bit more.

And ideally he so badly wanted to meet that cute boy again from the Christmas Party.

But Tony doubted that would ever happen.

***

Austin Jean stood in a long white corridor with posters on various things from charity events to student tips to everything in-between as he wondered about going to this *meet-up*.

It wasn't that he didn't want to go, he really, really did. He had always loved university for its amazing gay events and chance to meet other people like him.

Back in the tiny village Austin came from, the idea of meeting other gays was impossible, and it wasn't like his parents or anyone he knew was going to drive him to the train station an hour away, just so he could get a train to London and meet other gays.

That was never going to happen.

But Austin had worked hard, got a place at a university in a busy city and made sure there was an active gay scene there before he accepted the application. Of course he made sure not to tell his parents those details, but he was so glad he had come.

The sound of other students talking about assignments, dates and other nonsense echoed down the corridor as a large group of girls walked past Austin, and they didn't seem to notice him.

Austin just smiled at that. It seemed like no one really noticed him too much these days, maybe that was the way he liked it too. Austin had been very proactive in class, at gay events and everything he could throw himself into in the first two years of university.

But then this family found out he was gay over the Christmas break of the final year.

Austin knew it had been worth it going to that Christmas party, kissing that guy and then trying to find him on social media. But when his parents found him trying to *hunt down* a poor innocent guy, they really didn't see it like that.

Austin just shook his head as he saw a very tall guy he had met at other gay meet-ups walk past, clearly heading to the current one. Austin did want to go but he just wasn't sure if it was worth it.

They were always great fun, but Austin wasn't sure if that was him anymore.

Or rather more likely, Austin just wasn't sure if his parents found out going home would be worth it. That sounded so stupid to him, but considering his parents already doubted he was gay (and that made him furious) and simply thought he had been brainwashed into being gay at school, Austin just didn't know what to do with himself anymore.

He felt so invalidated and like this massive part of himself was just pointless. Because what was the point of being gay if you could never live it and have your family accept you?

Austin knew that there were tons of stories about gays being abandoned by their family, but he honestly loved them. His parents and brothers were great people, just not if you were gay, black or anything else that the Good Book said was criminal.

The smell of burnt coffee, horrible herbal tea and another strange hint of something just made Austin frown. There really wasn't any point subjecting himself to all that torture and temptation if he could never do anything about it.

After university Austin wouldn't be allowed to contact any of the amazing people from the meet-up again, he definitely wouldn't be allowed to bring a boy home and... there just was nothing going for him.

Not as long as he lived under his parents' roof, which considering how hard it was to buy a home these days, Austin sadly knew that he would be living at his parents for a long while to come.

And that was just damn well depressing.

The sound of a seriously cute laughter echoed down the corridor, and Austin couldn't help but feel like he recognised it.

He did.

Austin could have sworn he recognised it from

the Christmas Party and that really cute guy he had been kissing late that night. He made that laugh at a joke he made.

Austin really smiled and his entire body felt energised at just the idea of seeing that amazing guy again. Austin bit his lip and realised he seriously had to go to the meet-up, regardless of whoever else knew about it.

After going up the corridor, Austin went into the large university meeting room where the meet-up was happening, looked at all the great people he had met before and… shit!

Austin honestly felt like his heart stopped as he saw that same amazingly sexy hot guy from the Christmas Party, and now he was right in front of Austin, he was even more stunning.

Austin just loved the guy's utterly fit body with no fat or muscle, he was just fit. And Austin loved the guy's short brown hair that wasn't too long to do anything with, but it wasn't so short that Austin couldn't run his fingers through it, and that smile. This Stunning Guy had pearly white teeth that almost blinded Austin and he was on the opposite side of the room.

Stunning Guy was so perfect, sexy and just gorgeous.

Austin had to speak to him.

He had to get to know him.

And Austin really hoped Stunning Guy wanted that too.

***

After talking to a few gay men about how they were finding university, being gay and some tips about exploring this new part of himself, Tony had really surprised himself because of how amazing he was feeling.

He might have been nervous as hell about coming here, but now he was here. Tony couldn't deny how great this all felt to him and there were so many great looking guys here.

Sure Tony wasn't actually sure if these guys were as attractive as he felt, but he wondered if he was just so excited about being around so many men who were into the same things as him.

It was rather overwhelming in a great way.

And Tony had actually managed to talk to some Lesbians which Tony had never done before, and they were wonderful. All the stereotypes about them being manly, awful people was just flat out wrong.

They were great.

"Excuse me please,"

Tony didn't know why he heard that deep sexy voice so clearly considering all the other people were shouting, talking and playing a little bit of music all around him.

Then Tony realised that he recognised that voice. He had heard that the night of the Christmas Party and it was from that really cute guy, if he was here then Tony really wanted to find him.

And thank him for helping Tony realise who he

truly was.

"Excuse me,"

Tony turned around now that the sexy voice sounded a lot closer, and as Tony looked through the crowd he saw the most beautiful man he had ever seen.

A really cute man who was clearly about a foot shorter than Tony was slowly making his way through the crowd towards him. And Tony just couldn't believe how gorgeous he was, at the party it had been dark, loud and not exactly a great place to meet someone.

But now there were lights on, Tony was flat out amazed at the Cute Man's blondish hair that was combed upwards making him look adorably cool, sexy and just amazing.

And Cute Man had such a stunning pointed face with the dirtiest but most perfect smile he had ever seen and Tony just loved looking at him glide through the crowd towards him.

But he wasn't gliding anymore.

Tony quickly realised that Cute Man was standing, smiling right in front of him and Tony felt his palms turn instantly sweaty at the sight of such a perfect man.

"Um, hi," Tony said. "I'm Tony,"

Tony loved seeing Cute Man's face light up as he said his name.

Cute Man grabbed his hand and shook it. Hard. Tony forced himself to breathe as the shock, excitement and sheer delight shot through him at the touch.

"I'm Austin," the Cute Man said, and Tony forced himself not to do something silly at finally finding out his name.

He so badly wanted to punch the air in victory, but Tony knew that wasn't cool. He really had to stop acting and thinking like such a child, he needed to act cool.

"Tony's a… good name. I haven't seen you here before. Enjoying it?" Austin asked.

Tony so badly wanted to say it was so much better now he had seen Austin (that was a such a seductive name), but Tony was forcing himself to not seem too eager.

"Yea," Tony said, "it's great seeing other people. I've only just started knowing I'm gay. What about you? How long have you been gay or into men?"

Tony's eyebrows rose when he saw Austin's happiness, delight and excitement drain out of his face, and he looked furious at him.

Tony had thought that was a perfectly reasonable question but maybe it wasn't. He had a lot to learn about his new community.

"I'm sorry. Maybe that was too personal," Tony said.

Austin just frowned and walked away. His hands forming fists.

Tony placed his hand over his heart because he felt like he had just blown it with the most beautiful guy in the world.

And that just killed him inside.

Tony had one shot. And he just blew it.

***

A few hours later Austin threw himself onto the soft blue sheets of his bed in his little dorm room with the desk next to the bed and the bathroom just a few metres from the end of the bed. He felt so stupid.

All he had to do was talk and laugh and enjoy his time with that gorgeous Tony, but he just had to get defensive.

Tony was such a hot sexy man that was clearly interested in him, but Austin just couldn't get involved with him. Austin so badly wanted to, he wanted to talk, laugh and make love so, so badly with that man.

But one thought kept playing through his mind.

What would his parents say?

Austin hated himself and was furious with how stupid he had been. He could have just blown his only chance of happiness with such a great guy, all because he was scared.

All Austin's life he had been scared about one thing or another. The captain of the secondary school's football team wanted to go out with him of all people as soon as he turned 16 (which was 9 months later than the football captain) and that guy was great, and Austin loved how he had waited those nine months for him.

But Austin had gotten so scared then.

Then after secondary school and before university, Austin had been asked out by the smartest man in the entire year group. He was smart, funny and sexy and so perfect, but Austin had gotten scared because of his family.

No more!

Austin couldn't let Tony be the third person he let slip away because he was too scared to stand up for who he was, what he believed in and most important who he loved.

Austin forced himself to sit up on his wonderfully soft bed that smelt of lavender from the washing powder he used earlier. He just... he just wanted Tony. He just wanted to see where a relationship with Tony would lead, and not think about his parents, family and everyone else who doubted he was gay.

Austin took out his phone and dialled his best friend Kelly who also studied psychology, and considering she was the Student Representative for the course, who made sure she knew everyone and everything, Austin was really hoping she knew how to find Tony.

She thankfully answered on the third ring. "Hi Aus,"

"Hey Kel. You know everyone in psychology right?"

She laughed through the phone. "Darling, I'm Student Representative, it is my job to know everything. And I'm insulted you even doubt my ability to know everyone,"

"Great," Austin said, really not caring. "Where can I find Tony? I really need to see him. Please. Please Kelley tell me,"

Austin suddenly really regretted getting that desperate, but it proved how much he wanted to try a relationship with him.

Kelly went very quiet. "Is this Tony Marks? The guy you caused quite the stir with at the Meet-up earlier,"

Austin huffed. He really didn't want to become gossip round the university.

"I only ask because he called me too. He wanted to see if you were okay darling. In fact-"

Someone knocked at the door.

Austin put the phone down. He raced to the door.

But when he opened it, Austin almost wanted to shout and scream and cry as he saw it was just a cleaning woman from the university accommodation staff.

"Hi," she said, "just wanted to ask you if you wanted to complete a survey of my cleaning,"

Austin just frowned. He knew the cleaning woman and she was a wonderful darling of a person, but he really wasn't in the mood.

The woman smiled. "Can see you're not in the mood right now. Here's my card with a link on the back to the survey,"

Austin took it, smiled and thanked her. He just

wanted to throw it away, but when he turned the card over. There wasn't a survey link on the back, but there was a room number for someone in the building.

Austin just smiled.

He knew it had to be Tony, and he really, really wanted a relationship with him.

No matter what anyone thought.

Austin grabbed his keys and ran out the door.

***

Tony was so glad the amazing cleaning woman had offered to help him, after all he wasn't sure if Austin would want to see him, but now he sat on his velvety soft sheets of his large bed, next to his desk and bathroom was just by the door, he was starting to think he had made a massive mistake.

Tony heard someone walking up the corridor. It was just a group of girls leaving the floor.

Tony couldn't help but feel like he was just trying to pursue something that wasn't meant to happen. It was clear that Austin didn't want anything to do with him, so why did he feel the need to keep chasing it?

Maybe he should have just left Austin alone and learned to live with never experiencing being gay with him.

More footsteps filled the corridor then he heard laughing as a group of boys and girls walked by as they presumably got back from some lectures or something.

Tony just felt terrible. All he had wanted was to

talk, get to know and maybe kiss that stunning perfect Austin, but clearly that was never ever going to happen. And Tony couldn't spend the rest of his time at university getting excited at every sound of footsteps, just hoping it would be Austin.

Austin just wasn't interested.

Tony forced himself up off his bed and went over to his desk to start on some psychology coursework, there were some quiet and slow footsteps in the corridor, but Tony really didn't care now.

Someone knocked on his door.

Having no idea who it was, Tony went over and opened the door to be utterly amazed that a perfect stunning short boy was standing there smiling.

Austin looked so beautiful and probably even more than earlier, if that was possible.

"I'm sorry," Austin said.

Tony smiled. Now that Austin was here he really didn't care what had happened earlier, he only cared about what was going to happen now and what the future might hold.

"Can I come in?" Austin asked.

Tony nodded. He was still too amazed for words, so Austin came in and Tony shut the door, and the two of them just stood in the mini-corridor between the door and the foot of Tony's bed.

"I didn't mean to run off earlier. It's just my parents doubt I'm gay. They made me question myself, and I panic about bringing someone into that," Austin said.

Tony smiled. It was great to think about Austin was already starting to think about protecting him. That was sweet.

"It's fine. Really. I don't think my parents have quite got their heads around it yet," Tony said.

Austin smiled and both men just stood there for a moment, admiring each other's beauty.

"Can I ask it now?" Tony asked with a schoolboy grin.

"What?" Austin asked, giving Tony an evil grin. "Am I gay?"

Tony nodded. "Are you doubting yourself? Or are you gay?"

Austin smiled, kissed Tony and pushed him against the wall.

As Tony savoured the amazing softness and taste of Austin's lips, he had his answer, and as his wayward parts sprung to life, he had his answer about himself too.

He was definitely gay.

As Tony and Austin continued kissing, Tony just knew that there was no more doubt between them. Their chemistry, connection and love was definitely going to last, and Tony really, really looked forward to seeing where this went and where they would go to for the rest of their lives.

And just that realisation made Tony very, very happy.

LOVE IN HALLS

As he closed the cold wooden door and heard the lock click, Zach smiled a little looking at his small university apartment. Well, he said apartment but it was really just a room. A small long room with a high single bed without any sheets and a wonderful long wooden desk made from Beech wood. It was a wonderful colour.

Then Zach's eye went to the poorly yellow carpeted floor with all his stuff in boxes lying there just waiting there to be packed away. From his bedding to his cooking stuff to his textbooks and all the other university things your course tells you to have.

Admiring the plain white walls of his apartment, Zach felt the cold air flow past him as he realised his mother must have opened a window before she and Zach's father had left him. But the smell of harsh cleaning chemicals still filled the air.

As much as Zach loved the idea of coming to the University of Kent in the south of England, he was nervous. He only lived half an hour away by car but he still felt nervous. This was so new to him. Whilst he had been away from home before weeks at a time, they were always times with his friends and people who knew. He was here alone at university.

Of course, Zach knew university was meant to be a time of adventure, new discovery and fun but he hated parties. He never liked them so the idea of university had scared him at first. With Zach wanting to commune to and from university so he could still be with his friends and parents.

It was only when his best friend and the only person who knew he was gay mentioned that going and living at university would give Zach a chance to meet other gay people. Then he got more interested about living at university.

And in all honesty the university campus in historical Canterbury was beautiful, the buildings were clean, great and very fit for purpose. Especially, the law building that was great, except for the weird way the rooms were laid out. Zach knew it was going to be trying to navigate those corridors!

But now Zach was here at university, he wasn't sure if his plan to meet other gay people would work. He had tried to find out how to meet them online and Zach still didn't understand fully. There was an LGBT+ society (which was like a social group) but he was still nervous.

He was nervous about so many things but the feelings of loneliness didn't help. For the first time in his life, Zach felt completely alone at university and judging by the events on this week, so freshers could meet each other and socialise. Zach wasn't convinced his feelings of loneliness were going to ease.

In an ideal world that would be an opportunity for people who didn't like drinking and partying to hang out. A part of Zach was sure those places did exist but he didn't know how to find them!

And the massive thing that concerned Zach was what if his parents found out he was gay. They would absolutely hate him but Zach had tried to be the good straight boy for so long and his mental health had gone so many times. Was it so wrong Zach wanted to have fun and love whoever he wanted?

Zach wanted university to give him an opportunity to find out more about himself so bad. He just wanted to experience love and fun for once in his university life before he returned to his straight conservative family.

The sound of people running up and down the corridor outside but Zach smile for a brief moment. He knew he wasn't really alone and there were 7 other rooms in this area or the section of the corridor that he shared a kitchen with. He could easily find friends.

Looking back at his boxes of stuff and Zach opened one of the cardboard boxes. The cardboard feeling cold and smooth in between his fingers. When he saw the box was full of his cooking equipment, Zach took a deep breath and decided to go to the kitchen. He had to met new people and a part of him really hoped there was a hot (hopefully gay) guy here.

***

Looking at the small black chipboard table in the middle of the shared kitchen, Max had to smile at it. He had seen some awful university accommodations on the different opening days at different universities. But some of the worse places still had a good looking table.

But aside from that Max loved this kitchen, a row of reasonably large individual white cupboards went around the top of the kitchen at head height and another row was underneath the black chipboard worktops.

Smelling the horrid chemical filled air that left a pleasant lemony taste in his mouth, Max walked over to one of the large clear windows that went the entire length of the far wall. But you could only open the top windows.

Max thought that was sensible the last thing you wanted when they're having a party in the kitchen is have someone fall out the window. They were on the ground floor but still!

Max couldn't believe how excited he was about going to university. He was actually here after years of hard work, he was here at university studying economics.

He couldn't wait to go out and explore Canterbury from the historical cathedral to the museums to the student life. It was going to be great.

And Max had heard there was a great gay scene at all universities so he really wanted to go to that. A great chance to meet people and get to know other gays. (and maybe meet a boy for fun)

The closest Max had come to meeting other gay people were his school friends but Max just wanted to meet more. Because the problem with gay schoolfriends in the rural north of England is you can't experience wider gay culture. Which was another reason Max wanted, needed to come to a university near London.

Looking at his black plastic box of kitchen pots, pans and utensils on the wooden kitchen floor, Max didn't know where to begin. He had already filled his shelf in the fridge with his food and filled one of his cupboards with dry food.

Opening his white cupboard below the worktop, Max was surprised at the amount of space in it. He could definitely fit all his pots and pans in here and the utensils.

Pulling his plastic box over, the plastic feeling rough in his hand, Max started to put all the different things into the cupboard.

With his head buried in the cupboard trying to make a very annoying pot fit inside another one, Max heard the kitchen door buzz open, shut and another person walked in before stopping at the other end of the kitchen.

Max knew the polite thing to do was to stop and say hello to this new person straight away. But he wanted to make sure this pot fitted in the cupboard.

After a few moments it did and Max looked up and oh… Max was in trouble.

As he stared at this utterly beautiful boy with his back to Max wearing a pair of tight black jeans, a loose top that still highlighted how fit this boy was and his short blondish brown hair looked amazing.

A part of Max really wanted the Mystery Boy or man. It was the more appropriate term because they were all over 18 here. Max really wanted Mystery Man to turn around, he wanted to look at this man's face. It had to be beautiful.

Then Max started to notice the horrible chemical smell to the air had gone to be replaced with Mystery Man's strong beautiful earthy aftershave. He smelt great.

As his hands started to go a little sweaty and his head started to go light, the logical part of Max wanted to slap himself. He never acted like this not even around his insanely hot friend Callum at school. Max was a calculated, cool, outgoing student, not a constantly horny teenager.

But as Max admired this beautiful Mystery, he didn't care for what he was meant to be like. Mystery man was beautiful and if Max got the chance to spend the next year living near him then that was great.

Max's smile grew as Mystery man returned around to face him and Max got to look at his beautiful face. Those deep stunning rich blue eyes and his smooth perfect face all topped off by a boyish grin that made Max's stomach twist and turn inside.

After a few moments of looking at this beautiful Mystery Man, it dawned on Max. Mystery Man was staring at him and smiling. This could be great but he needed to make sure he didn't make it awkward first.

***

Pressing his small white key card against the large wooden kitchen door, it buzzed as it opened and Zach walked in. It was a bit of a challenge walking in holding a large cold cardboard box filled with kitchen equipment but Zach managed.

He couldn't believe that even the kitchen still stunk of the same harsh chemicals that his bedroom smelt of. But at least the kitchen left a strangely pleasant lemony taste in his mouth.

At first glance, Zach wasn't sure what he thought of the small shared kitchen. The wooden floor and black chipboard dining table in the centre of the room and the worktops were somewhat unexpected. Zach would have thought the chipboard would be covered up. Even if it was just covered with some plastic of some sort it would have looked better.

At least the shared kitchen had a great amount of

cupboard space as Zach walked up to his dedicated cupboards. Two large white cupboards, one at head height and the other below the worktop.

Looking at the other end of the kitchen, Zach smiled as there was another guy kneeling down to get into his cupboard.

Turning away so Zach could start to fill his cupboard with his own pots and pans, Zach started to feel excited for some reason. He supposed it could have been because the idea of going to university was finally hitting him. Zach could actually meet new people and socialise with new different types of people that his conservative family never would have let him socialise with.

That thought alone was enough to make Zach excited. He wondered what this new person was like and what he studied. As much as Zach appreciated most degrees he really hoped this man didn't do a boring degree.

But thinking that Zach smiled, a lot of people would have called his degree boring. Who wants to know about law? It's boring and Zach agreed to some extent. There were some boring parts of the law but it was amazing to be aware of the laws so you could use them.

Placing the last pot in his cupboard at head height, Zach felt like he was being watched so he made sure the final pot was safe inside (the last thing he needed was a pot jumping out at him) and he turned around.

Wow!

Zach instantly didn't know what to do as his stomach did flips and the butterflies inside him broke free. He didn't know what was happening.

Looking at this stunning, perfect guy in front of him, Zach didn't know what to look at first. He was so beautiful. The Flatmate had perfect light green eyes like emeralds that seemed to sparkle in the light and his slim frame was clearly a lie for a slightly muscular body beneath with a six pack. After years of PE classes, Zach knew the type of bodies that appeared not to be muscled but they were. The Flatmate was stunning.

It was all topped off by the smooth perfect blond hair parted precisely to the left, like all the Flatmate had done was swirl his head and it was perfect. He was so beautiful. And that movie star smile.

As Zach started to feel his heart speed up, he didn't know what was going on. He had never felt like this before but he had never seen a man as beautiful as Flatmate before. Was this normal?

Zach took a deep breath as he tried to understand what was happening to him. Was he attracted to Flatmate?

A part of him blamed his parents entirely for feeling like this, if they had allowed him to be who he was then he wouldn't be panicking about feeling like this now.

Then he realised Flatmate was also smiling back at him. Was he interested? Was he pleased? Was this a straight person thing to smile at another man?

Flatmate started to walk over to Zach, and he could smell Flatmate's sweet manly scent.

"Hi I'm Max," Flatmate said.

Max.

Zach smiled at the name alone. That was a great sweet name, a manly, perfect name.

Again Zach didn't know why he was making

such a big deal out of learning a name. But looking at Max, he really didn't care.

"Hey, I'm Zach,"

Max smiled and Zach felt a little flattered. No one had ever smiled at him like that before.

"What you studying?" Zach asked. It was a basic line, but it always worked at university.

"Economics. You?" Max said.

Whilst Zach had no idea what economics covered except the economy, he wanted to play it cool.

"Interesting. I'm doing Law,"

Max smiled at Zach. "You don't know a thing about economics do you?"

Zach looked to the floor for a moment. "Is it that obvious?"

Max placed his hand on the worktop and caught Zach's finger. Zach didn't want his finger to move as blood rushed to his head (and other places). It felt amazing. Then Zach realised he was so out of touch with himself. Was it normal to be so excited by a touch?

"Oh sorry," Max said, moving his hand away.

Zach frowned for a brief second.

"When did you get here?" Max asked.

"This morning. My parents had work so they didn't wanna make a day of it,"

"I'm sorry," Max said, clearly hearing the sadness in Zach's voice.

Zach felt strange another man saying that to him. The closest he got to another man saying something kind or gentle to him was years ago before secondary (high) school.

"It's okay. I'm sure they have some conservative

church stuff to do later anyway,"

Max leant forward, he was so close Zach would feel his body warmth and Zach savoured this sweet manly scent. Of course he wanted to kick himself for acting so weirdly or *gay* but he didn't care. A small part of him wanted his parents to see him like this. Not only because he was happy but because they would be so disappointed.

"They don't like gays," Max said with a boyish grin.

Zach smiled with a grin of his own. "Not one bit, why I wanna come to university. Get to meet some people,"

Max nodded and leant back. Zach's spirit fell a little as Zach moved away.

"I'm going to an LGBT+ event tonight. Not a party. Just a meet and greet. You should come. I'll be there. It be *nice* to see you," Max said, passing Zach a leaflet of where the event was.

Zach got the leaflet and stared for an extra few seconds into Max's beautiful green emerald eyes.

"See you tonight maybe," Max said as he picked up his black plastic box and left.

Zach looked at the little leaflet with where the meet and greet was, he wasn't sure whether to go or not.

***

Feeling the cold September evening air blow past him gently, Max stood outside a large white rectangular building with a rather nice looking grassy bit outside with a few blue flowers.

Max leant against the rough white brick wall as he pressed his back into it, he really wanted Zach to turn up. He wanted to see him and get talking to him some more.

They both felt their excitement and happiness when Max had honestly accidentally touched Zach earlier. But he was very glad he did it, maybe it was his mind trying to see if Zach was remotely interested. If that's what his mind was doing then Max needed to give himself more credit than normal. It had worked but Max just wanted to see Zach.

He wanted to look into those beautiful deep rich blue eyes and admire that stunning face. Even the thought of Zach made Max smile and his head went light quickly.

Breathing in the cold evening air that smelt refreshing and crisp, Max was a bit nervous. He had put his heart on the line for a beautiful but unsure man. What if Zach wasn't gay after all? What if he only thought he was but when it came down to it he was straight going through a phase?

Or even worse what if his parents found out and got angry at Zach? That was Max's true concern, it wasn't about himself but Zach. He was extremely grateful his parents loved him and accepted his *weirdness* as they joked. But Max was hardly blind to the fact other people weren't so lucky.

What if Zach got hurt too? Max frowned a little as he wondered if this was Zach's first relationship or love interest. It probably was, making Max a little unsure about if he should get with Zach if the opportunity came up. He wasn't sure if he was first material.

Sure a lot of boys had said Max was great and they loved him, but they still left him. They still abandoned him.

Looking out over the amazing university campus

with its wide open grass fields and wonderful white buildings with lots of other university students walking about with friends. The sound of laughter and chatting filled the air. Max smiled at their happiness and how these people were all coping with the move to university.

He honestly didn't know how Zach was going to cope especially with how Zach had sounded earlier. That beautiful man even looked a bit shy and nervous about meeting his flatmates for the next year. What if a meet and greet was too much?

A final burst of laughter from friends walking back or to god knows where made Max realise that he didn't care about his own feelings. He was definitely going to wait and see if Zach was coming. Max wanted Zach more than anything and he wasn't going anywhere. He was going to wait for him.

***

Walking towards the building with the meet and greet, Zach couldn't stop smiling as he slowly made his way there.

Feeling the cold, refreshing and crisp smelling air blow gently past him, Zach knew this was going to be the start of a great first year at university.

Looking ahead at the mini black tarmac road ahead of him, Zach knew it wouldn't be a long walk to the building and hopefully Max.

A part of him couldn't handle the thought of Max not being there. Zach wanted to see Max more than anything.

He almost laughed at himself as Zach remembered the panic and hurry he was in putting away all of his cupboard boxes trying to find clothes for tonight. Thankfully, Zach had managed to find a great freshly pressed white shirt that showed off his slim body and a pair of tight dark, dark blue jeans.

Judging by the reactions Zach had gotten from girls as he walked it seemed to be flattering. Zach hoped Max would find it attractive.

Continuing to walk towards the meet and greet, Zach started to walk a bend in the tarmac road as the road continued towards the group of buildings at the centre of the university campus.

A part of him was still shouting at Zach not to do this but that was the years or maybe even decade of forcing himself to be a good straight boy for his parents. But Zach just wanted a little taste of freedom tonight and maybe the rest of the university year.

What Zach really wanted was just to know what being gay was like. He wanted to experience what talking about boys was like and what one felt like.

Of course, Zach knew these thoughts sounded silly to other gay people, so he definitely wasn't going to tell Max. But to him these were so important, like a dirty little secret.

Zach started to turn onto the main university campus and in the far distance he could make out the amazing body shape of Max, and Zach stopped.

His stomach churned and the butterflies within him went crazy. Zach so badly wanted this but he hesitated.

What if his parents found out? What if he went to this meet and greet tonight and Max became his boyfriend? (Even the thought of that made him the most excited he'd ever been)

It surely wasn't right on Max to date him for a year, dump him when Zach went back home and blank him during Christmas and other times he went back home. That wasn't fair.

Hearing the other freshers laughing, chatting and being happy, Zach had to smile. All these amazing other people were happy and having a good time, so why couldn't he?

There was absolutely nothing stopping him and a year of being himself and truly being happy meant everything to him. And maybe it could give him the confidence to stand up to his parents if they ever found out.

Zach walked on.

After a few moments, Zach's mouth dropped at how beautiful and utterly gorgeous Max looked in his own very tight white shirt that showed off his amazing body and his six pack. (Zach knew he was muscular!) And Max's tight black jeans looked great too.

As soon as Max saw Zach he looked into Zach's beautiful eyes, Zach didn't care about what anyone except Max thought. So he gave him a massive hug. Pure magic and electricity filled them both as they hugged.

Zach breathed in Max's wonderful earthy, manly aftershave and held his hand.

Turning around and walking into the meet and greet, Zach knew for a fact this was going to be a great first year at university and hopefully a lot, lot longer.

GAY UNIVERSITY ROMANCE SHORT STORY COLLECTION

GAY, LOVE, HEIR

Feeling the cold wintery air brush over his cheeks as the wind blew gently, Stan kept walking up the long concrete path running up the hill to the university. Beautiful bright green trees lined the path and the sound of other students walking, talking and even cycling up and down filled the air as Stan kept walking.

He had one of his favourite classes that he wasn't going to miss for the world, he loved his biological psychology lectures. Stan just thought it was amazing how our biology could impact our behaviour in so many breath-taking ways. So he kept walking, he didn't want to be late.

As he walked he listened to the brief conversations of other students, they were all so glad to be back after the Christmas holidays, it was great to be back studying, learning and most importantly seeing friends.

That was something that Stan's parents never

quite understood about why he was excited to be back. He really wanted to catch up with his French and Spanish friends that had travelled back home for Christmas.

The smell of aftershaves made Stan smile a little as he saw some hot guys walk past as they left for the day. Stan supposed they were lucky with only having one lecture at the crack of dawn (9 am) but Stan still loved his midday lecture and then the rest in the afternoon.

When he neared the top of the hill, the path continued into the university grounds along wide open fields of lush green grass and Stan was filled with a sense of relief. He was back and he in a strange way, he was home. University had always been a home away from home for Stan, a home for learning, making friendships and maybe even finding love.

Stan's smile thinned a little as he wondered about finding love. Being gay at a university didn't sound hard in the slightest and he knew how fortunate he was to have the full support of his entire family (sometimes a little too much support!) but it didn't mean finding other gay people was easy.

Pushing those thoughts away, Stan continued to walk along the long concrete path that breathe in the fresh wintery air as the gentle wind flew past, and he continued to be more relaxed as he was back at university.

The place he belonged.

Knowing he had ages (tens of metres) to go

before he actually reached the university campus and even then it was a trek and a half to get to where his lecture was, Stan wondered what new students there would be today.

Even being in his first year at university Stan had made friends with some older students for hook-ups and apparently on the first day of the spring term (which Stan never quite understood because it was still January) new students would always turn up. Regardless of them being new domestic students or new foreign exchange students.

For some reason Stan felt his stomach fill with butterflies of meeting new people and potentially meeting new men. He smiled to himself as he knew at silly he was being. He studied psychology, human behaviour which was a female course mainly.

Stan's smile deepened as he remembered the jokes from his family about it was a shame he wasn't straight with all those women and it makes sense a gay should want to do what women do.

Stan still couldn't believe that they actually said about that but he agreed it was funny, and he did laugh.

But with psychology being a female-dominated course, it was rubbish for gay people. Stan never ever said that but he did think it. And to make things even worse, the men that were on the course were either straight or too straight acting to tell, and Stan had learnt long, long ago you never ask a man straight away if they were gay or not.

Still Stan really couldn't believe how silly his young self was.

But as he walked onto the university campus with the tall metal buildings around him, the air a strange mix of weed and fresh wintery air, Stan took a deep breath (coughed at the weed) and knew it was great to be back.

And this was going to be a great day. He just didn't know why.

***

With the sound of hundreds of students in all their different classes, heights and sizes talking, laughing and shouting around him, Robert pressed himself into a little corner of the white walled corridor as he waited for the lecture doors to open so he could go into his first lecture as an official university student.

Well, he had been a student at another place but… that didn't end up so well. So he came here to Canterbury, England and he hoped (he really, really hoped) things would work out better.

Breathing in the smell of expensive perfumes, aftershaves and some fresh air from the open windows, Robert looked down on the corridor and just couldn't believe how many students were here.

At his last university he was lucky to have another hundred or two in joined him in a lecture, but this was a lot more. It was easily three or four hundred students. Robert wasn't sure why the university designed this lecture theatre to be only accessed by a small corridor that was never ever going to fit hundreds of students at any one point.

Pushing those thoughts away, Robert pressed himself even tighter against the cold white wall as more students tried to pack themselves into the corridor. Robert wasn't a fan of the cold wall chill his back, he just hoped not all lectures were like this.

He didn't want a repeat of his last time, he just wanted a fresh start. A chance to make new friends, learning and maybe escape his life in the arms of a beautiful man.

Robert caught a laugh that almost escaped as he knew the last part was impossible. He was gay and proud and happy, but it seemed his happiness didn't matter, at least not in the eyes of his parents and wider family.

Robert rested his head against the cold wall allowing, willing the cold to chill his head as he remembered how he met a beautiful man at his last university and he was truly in love. He really loved that man. But his parents found out.

Robert bit his lip and frowned as he remembered how annoyed they were and how they threatened to cut him off and abandon him if Robert didn't change universities.

Listening to the sounds of more talking, laughing and shouting from his fellow students, Robert just stood there. He didn't want to think about the past, he wanted to learn and escape his home life, get a great job so he would never have to depend on his parents.

But his eyes wetted.

For some reason Robert knew that future was a long, long time away, and he hated how much longer he would have to deny himself what he loved and wanted to have fun experiencing.

Robert lifted up his head as he saw the massive group of students moving as it looked like someone or maybe more than one person was coming through the crowd. Robert leant forward as he wanted this to be the lecturer so he could get on with learning and forget about all his troubles.

But it wasn't.

It was just a group of students. Robert was about to look away when… his mouth dropped as he looked at the most beautiful man he had ever seen.

The Guy's beauty was staggering, it wasn't natural. Robert knew he was probably being silly but this Guy was… stunningly perfect.

Robert loved the Guy's tall slim body, sapphire eyes and his movie star smile. He was staggering, beautiful, perfect even. Robert quickly forgets all about his home life as he stared at this Guy with his staggering beauty.

***

When Stan turned the corner, he shook his head as he stared wide-eyed at all the students in all their different heights, classes and sizes who were just rammed into the little white walled corridor.

There was no reason for it but Stan was glad he

was still slightly early, he didn't even want to imagine what this crowd of students would be like if all four hundred students had turned up.

Normally Stan was early so he always missed these pre-lecture crams, but this was his first day back and clearly all the Christmas drinks and food had made him forget what university was like.

The smell of perfume from all the women was a little overpowering and it made the taste of faint chemicals form on his tongue, but Stan liked the smell, he really did. They were some great scents here and a part of Stan wondered if it would be weird to ask them what they were. He knew he couldn't tell them the perfume would be for him but he could just lie. The last thing he wanted was a rumour going round campus that he was really into perfumes and all the stereotypical gay things.

Forgetting about the perfume, Stan felt the cold air blow past him from the open glass windows and he looked at the crowd of students. He needed to get to the front to ask a question to the lecturer, he supposed he could talk to the lecturer after the lecture. But the Christmas drinks and food didn't fade the memory of how impossible that was after the talk as that's when everyone wanted to ask questions.

Stan knew he had to try another way.

As he focused on the massive crowd of students, Stan noticed there was a slight gap along the corridor where the full coldness of the windows would be felt. That was probably why no one was standing there yet.

Stan went for it.

He slowly glided through the massive crowd of students, his back cold as it touched the glass, and his nose filled the scents of perfume. Stan wanted to shake his head as he noticed a few students were following him as they all glided between the crowd and the cold windows.

After a few moments, Stan got to the front of the crowd and smiled to himself that he had finally got to the front. Now he could ask his question to the-

Stan's entire mind stopped as he looked at the only man in front of him. Stan's mind went blank as he stared at the beautiful man.

Stan couldn't quite understand what was so special or beautiful about the man, but he just was. Stan supposed it could have been the man's thin but strong jawline, bright seductive green eyes and longish blond hair. But this man was just beautiful.

Stan felt his palms turn sweaty and before he knew it he had walked over and he was standing just in front of the beautiful man in the little corner. Stan knew he had to say something but the man was still too beautiful and Stan's mind was still blank.

"Hi," the beautiful man said, sounding just as weak as Stan.

Stan's smile deepened as he listened to the man's smooth voice.

"I'm Robert," the man said.

Robert. Now that was a hot name.

Then Stan noticed that *Robert's* eyes were

gesturing him to speak, and Stan realised that he needed to introduce himself. It annoyed him a little how his mind wasn't working today.

"Hey I'm Stan,"

Stan instantly regretted his name as he realised how lame it must have sounded. It was nowhere near as hot and sexy as Robert. Stan just sounded silly.

But just as if Robert had read his mind, he said:

"That's a good name," he said biting his lip.

"Thanks, you new?" Stan asked.

"Yea I was at… another place before. I just got here today. It's ma first day,"

Stan's eyes narrowed a little. He could hear the sadness and regret in Robert's voice, he didn't like hearing or seeing this beautiful man in any sort of pain. Stan wanted to give him a hug or provide some sort of (physical) comfort to him but Stan knew that wasn't appropriate. Was it?

"I'm sorry," Robert said.

Stan really wanted to kick himself now. He wish he wasn't this easy to read, he didn't want Robert to think he was pitying or seeing him as someone to be cared for.

Stan opened his mouth but he didn't know what to say. Then he just decided to go with the classics.

"You okay?"

For a moment Stan didn't know if Robert was going to answer because he still stared at Stan, his eyes soft and… even longing for something that Stan didn't know. Maybe a friend, maybe someone to talk to, maybe something more.

The sound of the students falling silent and shuffling made Stan and Robert turn to see the lecturer coming down the hall and the lecture was going to begin soon.

Stan knew he had to offer something to Robert. He didn't know why, he didn't know why he was acting like this, but it didn't change how he felt.

"I'm going to library afterwards if you want someone to talk to," Stan said as the lecture opened the door and everyone went inside.

***

Sitting in the soft fold up chairs that were arranged level upon level like an amphitheatre in the lecture theatre, Robert stared at the PowerPoint that was on the large screen covering the wall in front of him.

He stared at it but he wasn't focusing on it, the PowerPoint was looking at the impact of hormones on behaviour and Robert couldn't concentrate enough to look at it.

As he felt the soft material of the chair between his fingers, breathed in the perfume and air conditioned scents and listened to the lecturer give a passionate talk about the topic, Robert couldn't stop thinking about Stan.

Robert was sure Stan didn't like his own name but he did. Stan was the sort of name that belonged to a manly man, a practical man, a hot man. Which Stan definitely was. Robert remembered Stan's staggering beauty and how badly he wanted to be with him.

Robert tried to focus back on the lecture but he couldn't. He could only think about Stan and how beautiful he was. Robert remembered his offer that Stan was going to be in the library later and he wasn't sure. He just wasn't sure.

As much as Robert wanted to talk to someone, he didn't want to inflict it all on Stan. Stan seemed like a nice, hot, perfect guy, he probably had all the men chasing after him and he didn't need Robert.

He hoped that wasn't true but Robert knew he was just making up an excuse not to go to the library. Granted he actually did need to go to the library to check out a few books he needed.

But he didn't want to do it if Stan was there.

Breathing in more of the perfume in the air, Robert remembered a very hurtful thing that his father (not dad. He didn't have a dad as far as he was concerned) had said again and again.

You must produce an heir to the family name.

Robert frowned as he remembered that saying and how hard and harshly his father had banged it into him ever since he was born.

And that was the real problem.

Watching the slides of the lectures change to show different cells and nerves, Robert realised that that was why his father would never accept him for being gay. Robert had to produce an heir for the family name.

Robert shook his head as he wondered about how stupid it was, so what if there wasn't a biological heir to the family name? Robert might have kids, him and his boyfriend might adopt, foster or go through surrogacy.

He knew he was going to be a great dad, he was great with kids and he was going to be a far better dad than his was. If his kids wanted to be a movie star, gay, straight, trans, whatever. That would be okay. Because Robert was going to love them, be there for them and support them no matter what.

Because that's what a good dad does.

A good dad doesn't force their child into a narrow path in life all because they want a child. And the only true way to get an heir is to have sex with a woman.

Robert realised his face was bright red and sweat was dripping down his back and wetting his neck. Sure he was annoyed but he needed to think about it and most importantly he needed to talk to someone.

Robert didn't like his parents for getting rid of all of his gay friends, his past boyfriends and anyone who could remotely corrupt their son and not deliver an heir. He couldn't believe his father had said gays are wrong because they can't have kids.

But as Robert looked across the lecture theatre, he stared at the staggering beauty, sapphire eyes and tall slim body of Stan. And Robert knew what he was going to do.

He was going to go to the library, talk about his

life with another gay person and live the life he wanted to live. His parents couldn't control him, how he felt or what we wanted.

And right now, Robert really, really wanted Stan.

***

Tucking the rough fabric chair in under himself, Stan smelt the amazing scents of bitter coffee, sweet cakes and citrusy oranges as he sat in the library café at a small two-person table as he waited for the most beautiful man he had ever seen to show up.

Stan looked around the busy café that was between the two massive halves of the library that was separated by a little glass door with lots of tables and students who were drinking, talking and laughing with each other.

Everyone was having a great time, a wonderful time, a perfect time.

But there was still no sign of Robert.

Stan felt his stomach tense as he wondered if Robert would show up. What if Robert didn't want to talk to him? What if Robert wasn't interested? What if Robert wasn't gay?

His eyes widened a little as Stan felt so silly for not even considering that. Stan almost wanted the ground to swallow him up as he wondered if Robert was actually straight and Stan had just made a massive fool of himself.

Then he breathed in more of the bitter coffee scented air.

Stan tried to just relax and enjoy the little break

away from the lectures before he went to his final one of the day. A part of him wondered if the final lecture (Human Sexuality) was some kind of plan from the universe to tell him to have a bit more faith.

But it didn't help.

Stan's stomach still felt tight and his palms were sweaty as he really wanted, needed Robert to turn up. He wanted to help him, he wanted to comfort Robert, he wanted to be with Robert.

Stan still wondered why he was acting like this, he never acted like a schoolboy who was head over heels in love before. But this time he felt different, he was different.

As much as Stan wanted to forget his feelings and focus on listening to Robert with whatever hardship he wanted to talk about, Stan couldn't. He couldn't forget how he felt, the things he wanted to say and do with Robert.

The sound of the glass café door opening made Stan turn around and his mouth dropped a little as he stared at the seductive bright green eyes, strong jawline and longish blond hair of Robert.

He was just beautiful. Stan didn't need any other words to describe him, he was just perfect the way he was.

Standing up Stan looked into those seductive eyes and Robert stared back, they both smiled and walked up to each other. They hugged.

And Stan loved the feeling of the pure chemistry and passion between them.

In that moment, Stan knew Robert was gay and he did care about him, and whatever happened today, Stan knew he was going to stay around, support him and be there for Robert for a very, very long time.

HOLIDAY, BURNOUT, LOVE

Benji Michaels had never been one for "falling in love". Lots of people often thought of him as too serious, focused on university and studying to have fun at parties, clubs and more of the partying side of university.

In truth, Benji never believed he was too serious. He only didn't like the drinking side of university. He loved people, hot guys and actually talking to everyone, but he hated with a passion the loud awful music that was pumped so loud he couldn't hear a person standing right next to him.

As Benji sat on the awfully uncomfortable fabric computer chairs at the university library at the very end of the massive row of computers on the top floor, Benji couldn't wait for the Christmas holidays to start in a few hours.

A lot of students had already left, but Benji still had one more biomedical science lecture to attend in the late afternoon before he could officially leave. All his friends had left yesterday, and as much as he wanted to join them. He was a tat too dedicated to his studies.

And as stupid as it sounded, Benji didn't want the poor lecturer to be all alone. If the lecturer was going to put the effort in, then Benji wanted to be kind enough to at least turn up.

The quiet mutters in the distance was the only sound despite the humming, vibrating and slightly popping of the old computers that filled the library. Lots of students would have been drained by the silence, but Benji wasn't.

Unlike other students Benji liked coming to the library for the quiet, it allowed him to concentrate, focus and actually achieve something.

Benji truly loved his parents and younger and older siblings at home, but they were a nightmare when he wanted to achieve something at home.

That's why Benji always came here on Friday afternoons.

The scents of strong flowery perfume with hints of cedarwood, pecans and cloves started to fill the air and leave the taste of Christmas cookies on Benji's tongue, strangely enough, and he instantly knew who was going to turn up sooner or later.

His best friend Victoria Harris always wore way too much perfume, but Benji didn't mind. Her attitudes and friendship more than made up for any problems the overwhelming smell caused.

The computer beeped as Benji opened up his

university emails and saw one from a slightly older university student. A senior, a year ahead of Benji, who Benji had to admit was very fit, hot and sexy.

Benji had always had a thing for Ezra Hawks ever since he had met him a few months ago when a professor Benji was helping out his year introduced them. Benji had no idea whatsoever if Ezra was into men, but he was hot.

All Benji could do was bit his lip at the idea of them two talking, laughing and spending time together.

As Victoria had said, they barely knew each other, but Benji had spoken to Ezra a few times and he always made Benji feel like a schoolboy, happy and alive.

Victoria tried to understand, but Benji knew she didn't. And he couldn't blame her, how do fall for a guy you barely know?

As Benji tried to forget about those doubts, he read the email and hoped it was a response to the work Benji had submitted to Ezra to get his opinion on. Since Benji was hardly the best student on essays (it was the so-called writing style that he struggled with the most) and he really hoped Ezra would want to meet up and give him some tips.

To Benji's frustration, Ezra had agreed to give some feedback but not in-person. Benji just smiled at his little attempt to see the hot sexy man in person, but it had failed.

But at the end of the day, Benji was just happy

for any guidance Ezra could give him.

Yet to Benji's surprise the email was rather coldly written compared to normal, and it was a very formal apology saying that Ezra didn't have time to give feedback this side of the Christmas holidays, and he would do it next year.

Benji finished the email and just felt like there was something more to it. He was partly glad that Victoria wasn't here yet because she probably would have said he was overthinking it.

But Benji had spoken, email and met Ezra plenty of times, and in every single email Ezra was a delight to talk to. Something else was going on, and even though Benji wasn't even friends with him, he still wanted to find out more.

As Victoria's heavy high heels pounded towards Benji, he just looked at the tall, beautiful brunette that was his best friend.

Thankfully she was good friends with Ezra and Benji really wanted her to do some spying for him.

***

Ezra Hawks had always wanted to go to university ever since he was a young teenager. He wanted to develop his knowledge, get a degree and get a professional job so he could help as many people as he possibly could.

That was one of the advantages of doing biomedical science. There were so many jobs you could do that paid very well and helped a lot of great people too.

But as Ezra stood in one of the university's many cafes with its rows upon rows of little tables, booths and a few other students sitting around. Ezra just wished he wasn't so committed to his studies, he wished he wasn't here anymore and he was home.

So many of his friends had already gone home and as much as Ezra wanted to do that. He felt like he wanted to do a lot more than just leave university for the Christmas Holidays. He was seriously considering giving up for good.

Ezra rather liked the scents of coffee, hot chocolate and cinnamon that filled the air as all other students bought their fuel to keep them going until the end of the university day.

Ezra stood holding his own hot chocolate and he was just enjoying the warmth radiating from it, and considering his future.

He had been working so hard so late. Reading as much as he could, working as much as possible on his dissertation and everything else that was expected of a first-class final year student.

And he hated it. Ezra had been throwing up from the stress for the past three nights. He hadn't been eating and he had lost half-a-stone recently too.

Ezra didn't feel rubbish, but he felt like that was a dangerous sign too.

Yet the most concerning thing of all of his troubles, was Ezra didn't have anyone to talk to. Ezra couldn't talk to his amazing friends because they were all doing great and loving life. He couldn't talk to his family because he didn't want to admit failure, and most of his family believed in it was first-class grades or nothing. And Ezra didn't want to tell his professors in case he looked bad.

Ezra was burned out, trapped and didn't know where to go.

A group of friends laughing as they walked out of the café made Ezra smile briefly. He wanted to do that with his friends but he knew sooner or later they would talk about their projects and he would feel terrible.

Ezra had felt bad enough emailing that sweet boy Benji earlier and telling him he couldn't look at his work this year.

Benji was such a sweet wonderful guy that Ezra did want to get to know better. There was something so innocent, cute and adorable about him. Ezra loved Benji's little button nose, boyish grin and stunning emerald green eyes.

And strangely enough, Ezra just felt so at home around him. Sure, he had only met Benji a few times, but he loved each of those times.

It was just a shame Ezra didn't feel like he could tell anyone, because he didn't want to be judged. And surely a relationship could never work out with Ezra perhaps moving to another university after his undergraduate degree?

"Hey Ez," Victoria said as she hugged Ezra.

Ezra was a little surprised to still see her here. He took Victoria for the type of girl that would leg it from university the second she could. But it was great seeing her.

Probably one of his only true friends.

"Thought you would have left yet," Ezra said.

Victoria weakly smiled. "Well I thought so to. I have a lecture later but wanted to skip it, but Benji convinced me to stay,"

Ezra forced himself not to shiver in delight as she said Benji's name. To his annoyance, because he never acted like this with anyone else, Ezra felt the urge to go to Benji, talk to him just so Ezra could feel at home and relax.

It was so strange how he could just do that so naturally around Benji. He didn't know why but he did.

"Is he okay about me not looking at his bits?" Ezra asked.

Ezra almost blushed about looking at Benji's *bits*. But he managed to stay professional, yet he'd been lying if he said the idea hadn't crossed his mind.

Victoria's smile deepened. "You know you can do no wrong in his eyes. He's sweet on you and you know it. And what's wrong?"

Ezra didn't want to hear about Benji's feelings. He wasn't sure he felt the same and he really didn't want to do anything that would end up hurting Benji later on.

"What you mean *up with me*?" Ezra asked.

Victoria forced herself to sigh.

"Darling Ez. Come on, you don't send Benji

formally cold emails. What's wrong?"

Ezra bit his lip. He didn't think he had been that obvious, but he really wanted to sound like he liked and was interested in Benji, just in case he felt the same.

Ezra wanted to kick himself for acting like this, maybe he was a lot more interested in Benji than he thought. But he couldn't get involved with him. Not with Ezra struggling with university.

That wasn't fair on either of them.

But maybe Victoria could help.

Ezra carefully took Victoria over to one side of the little café and told her about him struggling, being sick and not wanting to get Benji involved or hurt by a guy like him.

Victoria hugged him. "Benji might be good for you then. He likes you a lot. He might be some good stress relief if you get what I mean,"

Ezra really liked the idea of that, but he couldn't bring himself to do it.

And then Ezra just looked around the university café and realised he really didn't like any of this. He didn't like the university, the work and the rest of it, and he just wanted to escape it all for a little while.

Christmas was a week tomorrow so if he really wanted it, he could escape for a week and relax. He could go travelling, see the sites of England he had always wanted to see and there were always cheap deals around so it was possible.

Ezra really smiled at the idea of travelling. He

loved seeing different places, experience new things and it would give him the space to know what he wanted out of life.

"What?" Victoria asked.

Ezra slowly looked at her. "I'm going to travel for a week. I'll leave tonight and I'll know by Christmas what I want from my life,"

Ezra was hoping Victoria would look happy for him, but she didn't. Her face sort of dropped and Ezra instantly felt bad.

Victoria probably looked like that because Ezra had never been much of the spontaneous type. Normally he was an extreme planner, and the idea of him going travelling was probably unthinkable.

But it was what Ezra needed and as much as he loved her as a friend she wasn't going to stop him from doing this and making a decision.

And he told her so and kissed her on the head.

***

Benji stood up next to his computer on the top floor of the university library and stared out of the massive floor-to-ceiling windows out over the freezing cold campus. He really didn't want Victoria to tell him anything bad was happening, but he was really concerned about Ezra.

Without a shadow of a doubt Benji knew how silly he was for being concerned, because he barely knew Ezra at the end of the day. But he couldn't help but feel like there was a connection between them.

A connection Benji wanted to explore so, so

badly.

"We have a problem," Victoria said and she quickly told Benji about Ezra struggling of late.

Benji completely failed to hide his surprise. Ezra had always been so confident, hot and sexy whenever anyone spoke to him that Benji never would have imagined he was struggling with university.

"And I think he's going to quit university," Victoria said.

Benji's eyes just widened. "But Ezra has always wanted to help others. He wanted to become a first responder or paramedic. If he quits he would throw his life away,"

Benji was surprised at the small beads of sweat dripping down his face. He didn't want Ezra to do this, he wanted him to stay at the university and complete his degree.

He just knew that if Ezra left now then he would never forgive himself and Ezra would be doomed doing jobs he never wanted to do.

His life would be miserable.

But most importantly, Benji wanted Ezra to stay so he could see his beautiful face, amazing body and that killer smile that always made him feel so much better.

"How do I stop him?" Benji asked.

Victoria shrugged. "Don't know if you can,"

"I have to," Benji said, "I have to try. Ezra needs to stay. I…"

Victoria took a few steps closer. "I what?"

Benji focused on the small snowflakes that were starting to fall across the university campus.

"I... I care about him and I would never forgive myself if I didn't try," Benji said.

Victoria smiled. "Don't you think you're being a bit selfish?"

Benji threw his arms up in the air. She was being impossible.

"No!" Benji shouted. "This isn't about me. This is about all the people Ezra will never help,"

Victoria started laughing.

"What?" Benji asked.

Victoria hugged him. "That's how you convince him to stay, and I told him you're sweet on him,"

Benji rolled his eyes. He didn't want her to tell him that, and seriously, saying he was *sweet* on him made Benji sound so old. But maybe there was a point to this.

"How did he react?" Benji asked.

Victoria shrugged and started to walk away.

"He didn't my dear. And I have a train to catch and you have a man to save. Happy Christmas and see you in the new year Ben,"

As annoying as Victoria could be, he did love her as a friend. She could be mystic, uncaring and completely not dedicated to her studies, but she was probably the best of friends he could ask for.

And she was right.

Benji quickly packed up his things and raced off to find Ezra.

He had to stop him.

***

Ezra was really looking forward to travelling up to the lake district for a week to help clear his head. He was really looking forward to walking through the amazing hills, looking at the wonderful lakes and just being far from urban areas and in nature without another person around.

Ezra still smiled at what his parents had said earlier when he phoned them. They were proud of him for knowing what was right for him, they would love him no matter what or they were concerned about him.

He was concerned about himself too.

As Ezra popped open the booth of his little black car that was still parked at the university, he started to put his laptop inside and his stomach started to get tighter and tighter.

Ever since Victoria had told him that Benji liked him he couldn't stop thinking about it. Ezra loved how sweet, caring and great-looking Benji was.

He was almost tempted to ask Benji to join him for the week, but wasn't that wrong? Wasn't this week away meant to be about being alone and thinking about what was right for his future?

No. Ezra couldn't invite Benji.

His stomach tightened again as he closed the booth and the cold dampness of the weather increased as small snowflakes started snowing down. Ezra didn't know how cold it was going to get in the

Lake District, but at least he would be alone and able to think.

Before Ezra got in his car, he took a final look round the university and he wasn't sure if he would be back. He loved it here, he loved the learning and the people, but it just wasn't agreeing with him.

Ezra had already been sick again as he was coming out to his car (thankfully the bathrooms were close by).

The fresh vanilla scent from his car air refresher made Ezra smile as he got into his car, closed the door and started the engine.

He was leaving the university and he properly wasn't going back.

Ezra had to admit it would have been great to get to know Benji better, see him smile and even asked him out on a date. But Ezra couldn't bring himself to start a relationship with that sweet man if Ezra wasn't going to continue at university.

It just didn't seem fair.

Ezra looked about and started reversing out of the parking bay.

He hit something.

"Ouch!"

There was something so familiar and sexy about the person who shouted out, but Ezra quickly got out of his car and his hands covered his mouth when he saw he had hit Benji.

The cute sexy man was just laying there on the biting cold ground holding his ankle and hissing out in pain. Ezra lifted him up and Ezra loved the feeling of Benji's hard smaller body against his, and Ezra helped Benji into the passenger front side.

Ezra quickly ran round to the other side and he sat in the driver's seat.

"I'm so sorry," Ezra said.

After a few moments, Benji started laughing as the pain was clearly starting to ease off.

"It's probably my fault too. I sort of race out to get you before you left,"

Ezra rubbed his eyebrows. He couldn't believe that Victoria ran straight to Benji, the very man he was trying to spare the feelings of. He didn't want to do this but he was clearly going to have to be straight with such a beautiful man.

"Benji I-" Ezra said.

"Wait. Listen," Benji said. "I know you're struggling but you'll pass. That's all that matters. You don't need to be a first class student for everyone, all you have ever wanted to do was help people and become a paramedic or first responder,"

Ezra nodded. He didn't know why he had forgotten that, he had been so focused on pleasing his parents and family that he had forgotten why he was doing this in the first place.

Benji hissed as he moved his ankle and he leant closer to gently rub Ezra's hands. Ezra couldn't believe how amazing it felt to have Benji holding and rubbing his hands.

"And all I want for you is to be happy and do

what you want with your life. Even if you don't want me," Benji said.

Ezra didn't know what to say.

Of course he wanted to go out with Benji, see what their relationship would bring and everything and it was amazing that he actually cared about Ezra as much as he did.

Ezra just…

Benji kissed him. Ezra loved the amazing softness and sweetness of his lips against his.

Then Benji pulled away and gestured that he was getting out of the car.

"Sorry. Just wanted that in case you do leave," Benji said.

Benji popped open the door but Ezra grabbed his hand. Ezra couldn't leave the university, his future or this beautiful man without at least trying out a relationship.

And Ezra couldn't think of a better way to test out a relationship than going away together. He had already paid for the room and it did come with a large double bed.

"Come with me. Please," Ezra said.

He was expecting Benji to say no, leave him and protest something rotten.

But he just smiled, got back in the car and kissed Ezra again.

It was the first of many passionate kisses before they left the university car park.

***

On their last day of their little holiday together Benji stood outside their little wooden hut in the middle of nowhere in the freezing cold. The air was wonderfully crisp with hints of damp, coldness and pine that was so delightful to breathe in.

Benji had left Ezra sleeping in their sensational double bed that had plenty of use over the past week, and Benji actually couldn't believe how perfect the last week had been.

Benji had absolutely loved talking and hiking and exploring with Ezra about everything that they wanted to achieve, their families and the rest. They had both laughed plenty of times about how similar they were, they both grew up in similar places and they just had so much in common.

In one week they had felt such a strong connection to each other, and that connection had only grown in the past week. Benji was really looking forward to the future that they would make together, and that was definitely true.

And thankfully both Benji's and Ezra's families had video called their sons over the holiday so they got to briefly met each other. Benji loved Ezra's family because of their liveliness, energy and personalities. And they loved him according to Ezra.

It was the same for his family.

As Benji felt two wonderfully strong arms wrap around him from behind, he kissed Ezra's arms and turned around. Benji loved Ezra in his posh grey jumper and wonderfully styled hair that Benji had messed up plenty this week.

And they both smiled at each other like lovers and schoolboys do.

Because this was going to be the start of an amazing final day of their holiday, and the start of something much, much longer.

But just as special. If not more so.

GAY UNIVERSITY ROMANCE SHORT STORY COLLECTION

UNIVERSITY, STUDENTS, LOVE

Jesse felt the cold metal chair under him pulse chills up his spine as he sat there, nursing his large white coffee and waited for his meeting.

Looking around the café, Jesse couldn't believe how great it was to be back on university campus after the summer break and a few months of things being online due to strikes.

It was great to be back on university campus around people his own age and admittedly hot guys once again. Jesse had forgotten how he missed seeing different people over the summer besides his friends and family.

There was always such a buzz and atmosphere at university that made you forget what was going on outside and made you focus on the amazing university environment.

Even the café was a great example of this, Jesse loved the modern bright design of it with rows of little black tables and metal chairs. It made the café feel large, comfortable and even a little posh too. Which as a university student that made him feel good about his budgeting.

His eyes narrowed on the centre ring of black (chipboard) marble and the sterile white of the counters with an impressive array of sweet treats there to entice people to buy more whenever they ordered their coffee.

Granted Jesse was only looking at it again because the tall Italian blond was really good looking, but Jesse knew from conversations with his best friend who worked here that he was straight.

Breathing in the strong smell of coffee, sweet cakes and some fruity teas, Jesse listened to the gentle mood music that played ever so quietly in the background, only adding to the atmosphere of this amazing café.

Then he turned his attention to the meeting at three o'clock and dreaded social afterwards. The meeting part was simple enough and he knew he was going to love it, but it was the social he was dreading.

As a placement student in psychology, Jesse loved doing his year's work experience working with a professor doing psychology research. He'd been doing it for two months now and it was great, he got to do it from home so he could do other things around it. Which suited him perfectly.

Jesse wasn't exactly sure what this meeting was about today but he didn't mind, he knew nothing would change dramatically and this was properly just a formality.

But after the meeting there was a university social.

Jesse had always considered himself a sociable person, he loved going out with friends, family members and watching football games. It was fun and he loved having fun.

But university socials were something else.

From everything he had heard university socials were about drinking, clubbing and everything in between. Jesse didn't want to do that, he didn't like it but he had to go, and as much as he loved wriggling out of situations, he knew he couldn't on this occasion.

A part of Jesse was glad that his friend Tom was going but Jesse still felt uneasy about going to it. What if the social was what he feared?

Then he reminded himself that things weren't always as bad as he imagined, and there was one person who he wouldn't mind seeing for longer.

Roman.

Just thinking of him made Jesse's stomach fill with butterflies and do little schoolboy flips. He really, really liked Roman.

Granted he had only seen him on Zoom meetings a few times, Jesse still thought of him as cute, and it didn't help his feelings when he found him on Facebook and saw some pictures he was in. Roman was even cuter in those photos than Jesse thought possible.

So to say he was looking forward to seeing Roman in real life was an understatement.

Breathing in the smell of strong coffee, sweet cakes and fruity teas, Jesse looked at his watch and smiled as it was almost three o'clock. Roman would be here soon.

And that excited him more than anything.

***

Feeling the cold coffee-scented air around him, Roman walked through the large brown corridors of the university towards the café where his meeting was meant to be.

After walking all this way from his office (well it was Professor Karen's actually but he used a desk in it) to the little café, Roman was starting to question the wisdom of not carrying his laptop in its bag. His arms were starting to grow a bit tired, but that could have just been because of who the meeting was with.

He looked at all the posters and corkboards on the walls as he passed and shook his head at their array of topics. Some were about university societies, others were school of psychology related and others were just random.

Listening to his light footsteps echo around the empty corridor, Roman took deep breaths as he kept walking. He didn't like the fact he was nervous, he knew he was going to have Doctor Karen next to him, but Roman was still nervous.

But he couldn't afford to tell anyone why he was nervous.

He had only seen Jesse a few times on a badly pixeled Zoom calls but even then Roman still thought he was hot. He was beautiful on a zoom call, who manages that?

Roman had given up trying to look good on online video calls because it was flat out impossible. No one could ever do it, so why should he? That was all until he had his video calls with Jesse, and Roman was honestly impressed he had managed to act professionally during the meeting. It was a struggle having to look at all that beauty for ages.

But Roman managed.

(Even if he did have to turn off Jesse's camera without him knowing once or twice)

Turning a corner Roman came out onto another long brown empty corridor but he could hear people talking, laughing and walking in the distance so he knew he was coming up to the café. The smell of bitter coffee was stronger too.

Attempting to turn his thoughts away from Jesse, he remembered what was the point of the meeting. It took him a moment because his mind kept going back to Jesse but Roman knew it wasn't anything important. It was just about seeing if Jesse was okay, enjoying the placement and moving forward.

Moving his laptop to another arm, Roman's eyes widened when he looked at his black, blue and grey nails that swirled together in a stunning design.

Roman stopped walking. What if Jesse didn't like feminine men? What if Jesse didn't like Roman? What if he wasn't gay?

Then Roman mentally kicked him. He hadn't even met the guy yet and he was getting nervous about it for nothing. He just needed to help Professor Karen with the meeting, talk to Jesse and be professional.

How hard could that be?

Roman kept walking, reached the café and open its door.

Then he knew he was screwed as he stared at Jesse. He was even more beautiful than Roman imagined. On the video calls, his face always looked a bit uncared for with stunning eyes and beautiful hair.

But in reality, he was just so, so hot. Roman loved Jesse' movie-star face with slim cheeks, strong jawline and stunning sparkling sapphire eyes. Roman would have been perfectly happy to just stare at it all day.

Roman forced himself to look away, but he couldn't. Roman marvelled at Jesse's amazing short dirty blond hair and despite Jesse sitting down, Roman had to admit he looked fit in that tight jumper.

Again he mentally kicked himself. He was a PhD student for Professor Karen, he needed to be professional and alert. He couldn't keep smiling and acting like a schoolboy around Jesse.

But he was so hot.

Hearing the door behind him open and close, Roman turned around to see a tall woman in a long black coat and black hair. Professor Karen.

"Ready Roman?"

Roman walked over to the table with Jesse, and he hoped he wasn't going to screw this up. But if nothing else at least he got about an hour to stare, admire and marvel at Jesse.

***

Jesse's stomach filled with butterflies again when he saw it was three o'clock and Roman and Professor Karen would be here at any moment.

Breathing in the amazing smells of coffee, fruit teas and sweet treats, Roman had almost forgotten about Professor Karen, a brilliant social psychologist who focused on conspiracy theories and an idol of Jesse's. He still felt bad for almost forgetting that she was coming but no one could blame him for thinking of Roman too much.

Taking a sip of his lukewarm coffee, Roman loved the amazing bitter flavours with hints of honey, nuts and peppermint that exploded in his mouth. It tasted amazing!

After a few more moments of waiting, Jesse started to wonder about what he would be like with Roman sitting close to him.

Then he panicked.

What if he said the wrong thing? What if he embarrassed himself AND Roman? What if Roman wasn't gay?

Jesse smiled as he took another amazing slip of his coffee as he realised that the problem with being gay in a straight world. He swore gays had it harder than straighter people for finding love.

Straight people only needed to see a woman then chances are she's a possibility, then the straight man can start the relationship and all that courting as his grandparents called it.

Gay people. They see a man but that means nothing. He's probably straight, loves women and gays can only admire them from afar. Meaning gay people need to spend at least three times longer trying to find a possible man before any of that courting (he couldn't believe his grandparents still called it that) could begin.

But he loved men, being gay and being proud of it.

Looking around the café with its little black tables and metal chairs and listening to the music in the background, Jesse took a deep coffee-scented breath and promised himself to act professionally, not to screw up and remain calm.

Hearing the café door open, Jesse looked up and swore under his breath as he knew that was going to be damn well impossible as he saw Roman (in person) for the first time and he was…

Jesse didn't actually know. He wasn't his normal type of dead drop gorgeous but there was just something about him.

Jesse couldn't help but smile as he looked at Roman's beautiful brown poofy hair that looked amazing, his slim fit body and his smooth round face with a little mini-beard growing out.

He didn't know what it was but there was just something so beautiful about Roman. He was even more beautiful than his pictures and video calls.

Jesse had to talk to him.

Hearing the café door open again, Jesse's smile lessened a little as he saw a tall woman with long black hair and wearing an even longer black coat walk in, and Professor Karen waved at him and said something to Roman.

Watching them both walk over, Jesse tried to focus on both of them equally but his eyes kept flicking back to Roman. Jesse was trying to work out what was so beautiful about him, but he couldn't. Roman was beautiful, there were no reasons for it, he just was.

When they both sat down, Jesse said hello and did the normal introductions to Professor Karen and Roman. But Jesse's mind was really focused on Roman as he got out his laptop and set it up.

"Whilst Roman sets up his laptop, how are you finding the placement so far?" Professor Karen asked.

Jesse forced himself to look away from Roman.

"Good thank you. I'm enjoying it and it is interesting work. Especially on the literature review,"

"Definitely. The articles you're finding are really good and you're actually helping me with some of my final year students," the Professor said.

Jesse looked at Roman again before returning to the Professor.

"Great what are they working on?" Jesse asked.

"You'll love this, one's working on how personality affects a person's vulnerability to conspiracy theories. And another is focusing on improving group relationships by combining some approaches I've conducted research on,"

As the conversation continued, Jesse kept flicking between the Professor and Roman, he wanted to moan at himself because he knew he shouldn't have been acting like this, but it felt so right.

He loved looking at Roman's poofy hair and amazing face and body, he looked so beautiful. And Jesse's butterfly filled stomach, sweaty palms and reddening face didn't help him too much.

"You okay Jesse? You seem a little red," Professor Karen asked.

Jesse wished the ground would swallow him up, but he saw Roman look up from his laptop and smile at him.

He wasn't sure how to take that but if the Professor (the person who was in charge of his placement) was picking up on things, he knew he had to try and control himself.

"Yes sorry Karen, I'm a bit hot. Do you mind if I take my jumper off?" Jesse asked.

"Of course not. I better take my coat off too," the Professor said smiling.

As Jesse took his jumper off, he looked at Roman a couple of times, and to his surprise he was smiling, biting his lip and his eyes were locked on

Jesse.

Jesse didn't know how to take that, he wanted it to be a sign that Roman liked him, but Jesse reminded himself to be professional and try not to look like a loved up schoolboy in front of the Professor.

As the Professor started to talk about the experiment and things moving forward, Jesse noticed Roman's nails. They were a beautiful mixture of black, blue and grey. They were beautiful, just like Roman.

And for the first time ever, Jesse felt like he wanted to paint his nails. He had never been interested in any of the stereotypical gay stuff, he had had lots of friends and boyfriends who liked nail polish, pink and feminine jewellery, but that stuff didn't do anything for Jesse.

Until now.

Jesse smiled briefly as he knew that he had no reason (probably) to be worried that Roman wasn't gay, or at least a little bit inclined.

After a great meeting that Jesse loved because the experiment, everything moving forward and spending more time with Roman sounded great. The Professor shook Jesse's hand and made him promise he was going to be at the social tonight.

Jesse was definitely going now.

Professor Karen put on her long black coat, told Roman to meet her in her office and left.

Jesse stood up at the same time as Roman and they stared into each other's eyes and smiled. Jesse knew this was weird and strange as his stomach did little schoolboy flips but Roman was so beautiful.

"I'll see you later then," Jesse said biting his lip.

Roman shook Jesse's hand, Jesse loved the little explosion of sparks between them.

"I look forward to it," Roman slowly said, also biting his lip.

After Roman had gone, Jesse collapsed into his chair, feeling weak, sweaty and lightheaded. The rest of his placement was going to be hard if he kept having to see Roman every day.

But he wouldn't have it any other way. He just hoped Roman felt the same way.

***

Stepping into Professor Karen's small office with two desks and a filing cabinet that Roman didn't like, he breathed in the amazing scents of Karen's flowery perfume and he listened to the sounds of keyboard tapping, students walking in the corridor and the howl of the wind outside.

As Roman looked at Karen who was typing away, smiling, and still wearing her long black coat, he wondered what she was smiling about. He knew she always smiled and was a happy person, it was one of the reasons why he wanted her as his supervisor for his PhD, but this smile was different.

Sitting on his cold desk, Roman tried out to react as the cold shot up him and he stared at Karen, waiting for her to say something.

He was going to have to wait until the social or

wait until he passed out from her flowery perfume that was growing stronger and stronger by the second.

After a few moments, Karen finished whatever she was typing, closed her laptop and looked at Roman, smiling.

"Sorry about that I was starting the introduction to our new paper," Karen said. "I thought you would take a bit longer with Jesse,"

Roman's eyes narrowed on her, noticing her smile was getting bigger.

Roman looked at the door, making sure it was shut.

"Why?"

"Come on Roman, I saw the way you two were staring at each other. I'm surprised the entire café didn't notice,"

Roman bit his lip.

He didn't want Karen to think less of him, what if she reported him to HR? What if she was concerned about safeguarding? What if? Roman knew he had to reassure her.

"Professor I can-"

Karen laughed a little. "Ro, how long have we known each other?"

Roman shrugged.

"I taught you for three years during your undergrad, a year for your masters and I'll be your supervisor for the next four years for your PhD,"

Roman didn't know where she was going with this.

"Ro, I'm saying I know you. I've known you for basically five years at this point, and what I saw today was…"

Roman wished the ground would swallow him up, he didn't want her to say unprofessional, indecent or any other word that could get him kicked out.

"Great. That's the first time I've seen you truly happy. Sure you've had boyfriends in the past five years, but you have never looked at them or spoken about them how you look or talk about Jesse,"

Roman had no idea what to say. It didn't sound like she was condemning him, but what if this was a test?

"It's not like this I-"

"Ro, you're scared. I get it. But as an unofficial friend please don't let you suppress these feelings forever,"

"But the university," Roman said.

Karen nodded, swiped her laptop a few times and showed something to Roman. When Roman got closer it looked like some documents about Jesse's placement, it was. These were the HR document that Karen had to sign for the safeguarding and paperwork side of the placement.

(Something Roman was glad he never had to do)

Karen pointed to some names at the bottom.

"What does that name say? And the position,"

"Professor Karen, Placement Supervisor," Roman said.

Karen nodded. "As far as the university is

concerned I am in charge of Jesse and his placement. You are just another student under my supervision. Yes, work together. Every PhD student and supervisor work closely together,"

Roman started smiling.

"Yes you have two? Three?" Karen said, and Roman knew where she was going with this.

"Three," Roman said.

"Three teaching sessions a week. Still in the eyes of the university, you are not a teacher, not in a position of power, not anything. You are just a student like Jesse. And guess what relationship can happen between students?"

Roman bit his lip and looked to the floor.

"Of course Ro, just to be on the safe side I probably shouldn't know of a relationship if it happens. But I don't care, as long as you both get the work done, I really don't know. I like you, I like Jesse, you're both great students and will be great psychologists one day,"

Roman kept looking at the floor, breathing in Karen's flowery perfume and listening to the howl of the wind as he wondered about what she had just said.

His smile grew as he thought about how beautiful, hot and stunning Jesse was, he was amazing and the way he took his jumper off… that was hot.

As his face reddened, Roman didn't want to push these feelings away anymore, he wanted to act on them, but he still wasn't sure. He believed Karen about the university's likely position if they found out but there was something still nagging at him.

Then he realised and laughed a bit, he wasn't concerned about himself, he knew he was fine, he was a successful student and had Professor Karen to support him.

But Jesse didn't.

That's what he was concerned about, Roman was worried if something bad could happen to Jesse, would the university not be so kind to him? Roman couldn't let that happen.

He looked back at Karen who was still smiling at him.

"You want me to do this, don't you?" he asked.

"Believe me, I'm over 40 and... I looked at a man like you do towards Jesse. I wish I'd taken a chance. Please don't make the same mistake,"

Roman smiled and nodded. He was going to spend the night with Jesse at the social, he was going to learn more about him, stare at his stunning eyes, hair and face and maybe ask him out.

Roman smiled at that idea, he was definitely going to ask him out, maybe to coffee, maybe something stronger, maybe even dinner.

And if nothing happened beyond that, that was fine because he had taken the chance and that's all he wanted.

***

Looking at his watch, Jesse felt a wave of nervousness wash over him as he knew it was almost time for the social, even with that beautiful Roman there, Jesse was still nervous.

Jesse started to walk down the long brown corridor with little random posters and announcements on the walls as he went to the room where the social was being held.

Breathing the smell of strong bitter coffee from the café nearby, he felt his face reddened, his head go light and his stomach flip as he thought about staring and being close to Roman for so long. It would be unbearable being so close but so far from what he actually wanted.

As Jesse heard the talking, laughing and loud footsteps of other students, Jesse wondered if he shouldn't go. Sure he would have to explain himself later to Professor Karen, but at least he wouldn't have to sit there for hours, talking, smiling and admiring Roman without being able to do anything about his feelings.

He was going to have that for the rest of the academic year, working side by side with such a perfect, beautiful man that in itself was going to be great but difficult.

But Roman did like him.

When he remembered how Roman's brilliant eyes looked at him normally and how he stared at him when he took his jumper off, Roman had to like Jesse.

He knew that but would he really risk himself in the eyes of the Professor and the university just for a mere boy like Jesse. Jesse didn't know but he wished Roman would.

Continuing to walk down the corridor, Jesse smelt scents of fruit teas in the air knowing (from other students) Professor Karen loved to bring them to socials, even now he could taste their sweet fruitiness on his tongue, sweat started to roll down his back.

Jesse stopped and stood there for a moment.

He so badly wanted Roman, he wanted to run his fingers through his beautiful poofy hair, stare into those brilliant eyes and do lots of things with him. But Jesse was scared.

He didn't want to get hurt and he didn't think he could handle getting rejected from such a beautiful guy such as Roman.

Jesse went to turn and walk away when he realised the worse thing that could happen during the social was he could have to admire Roman's beauty from afar for a few hours.

There was nothing bad about that.

So Jesse kept walking down the corridor, turned left into a large white-walled room. It was perfect for a social with all its large tables and chairs for sitting around.

When Jesse looked around, he knew there were other people there but he saw the only person he needed, Roman was sitting there, looking right at him and he gave Jesse a schoolboy grin.

In that moment Jesse knew no matter what

happened tonight he was going to ask Roman out and hope, pray, whatever that Roman would say yes and whatever their relationship turned into it would last a long time, hopefully past the end of the academic year and into the far future.

When Jesse stood Roman continue to look at him with his little schoolboy grin, Roman pulled out the chair next to him and Jesse went straight over.

Jesse knew his and Roman's future together was looking bright, and that things were going to be good for a long, long time.

GAY UNIVERSITY ROMANCE SHORT STORY COLLECTION

GET YOUR FREE AND EXCLUSIVE SHORT STORY NOW! LEARN ABOUT NEMESIO'S PAST!

https://www.subscribepage.com/fireheart

About the author:

Connor Whiteley is the author of over 60 books in the sci-fi fantasy, nonfiction psychology and books for writer's genre and he is a Human Branding Speaker and Consultant.

He is a passionate warhammer 40,000 reader, psychology student and author.

Who narrates his own audiobooks and he hosts The Psychology World Podcast.

All whilst studying Psychology at the University of Kent, England.

Also, he was a former Explorer Scout where he gave a speech to the Maltese President in August 2018 and he attended Prince Charles' 70th Birthday Party at Buckingham Palace in May 2018.

Plus, he is a self-confessed coffee lover!

OTHER SHORT STORIES BY CONNOR WHITELEY

<u>Mystery Short Stories:</u>
Protecting The Woman She Hated
Finding A Royal Friend
Our Woman In Paris
Corrupt Driving
A Prime Assassination
Jubilee Thief
Jubilee, Terror, Celebrations
Negative Jubilation
Ghostly Jubilation
Killing For Womenkind
A Snowy Death
Miracle Of Death
A Spy In Rome
The 12:30 To St Pancreas
A Country In Trouble
A Smokey Way To Go
A Spicy Way To GO
A Marketing Way To Go
A Missing Way To Go
A Showering Way To Go
Poison In The Candy Cane
Christmas Innocence
You Better Watch Out
Christmas Theft
Trouble In Christmas
Smell of The Lake
Problem In A Car

Theft, Past and Team
Embezzler In The Room
A Strange Way To Go
A Horrible Way To Go
Ann Awful Way To Go
An Old Way To Go
A Fishy Way To Go
A Pointy Way To Go
A High Way To Go
A Fiery Way To Go
A Glassy Way To Go
A Chocolatey Way To Go
Kendra Detective Mystery Collection Volume 1
Kendra Detective Mystery Collection Volume 2
Stealing A Chance At Freedom
Glassblowing and Death
Theft of Independence
Cookie Thief
Marble Thief
Book Thief
Art Thief
Mated At The Morgue
The Big Five Whoopee Moments
Stealing An Election
Mystery Short Story Collection Volume 1
Mystery Short Story Collection Volume 2
Criminal Performance
Candy Detectives
Key To Birth In The Past

Science Fiction Short Stories:
Temptation
Superhuman Autospy
Blood In The Redwater
All Is Dust
Vigil
Emperor Forgive Us
Their Brave New World
Gummy Bear Detective
The Candy Detective
What Candies Fear
The Blurred Image
Shattered Legions
The First Rememberer
Life of A Rememberer
System of Wonder
Lifesaver
Remarkable Way She Died
The Interrogation of Annabella Stormic
Blade of The Emperor
Arbiter's Truth
Computation of Battle
Old One's Wrath
Puppets and Masters
Ship of Plague
Interrogation
Edge of Failure
One Way Choice
Acceptable Losses
Balance of Power

Good Idea At The Time
Escape Plan
Escape In The Hesitation
Inspiration In Need
Singing Warriors
Knowledge is Power
Killer of Polluters
Climate of Death
The Family Mailing Affair
Defining Criminality
The Martian Affair
A Cheating Affair
The Little Café Affair
Mountain of Death
Prisoner's Fight
Claws of Death
Bitter Air
Honey Hunt
Blade On A Train

Other books by Connor Whiteley:

Bettie English Private Eye Series
A Very Private Woman
The Russian Case
A Very Urgent Matter
A Case Most Personal
Trains, Scots and Private Eyes
The Federation Protects

Lord of War Origin Trilogy:
Not Scared Of The Dark
Madness
Burn It All

The Fireheart Fantasy Series
Heart of Fire
Heart of Lies
Heart of Prophecy
Heart of Bones
Heart of Fate

City of Assassins (Urban Fantasy)
City of Death
City of Marytrs
City of Pleasure
City of Power

Agents of The Emperor
Return of The Ancient Ones
Vigilance

Angels of Fire
Kingmaker
The Eight
The Lost Generation
Lord Of War Trilogy (Agents of The Emperor)
Not Scared Of The Dark
Madness
Burn It All Down

The Garro Series- Fantasy/Sci-fi
GARRO: GALAXY'S END
GARRO: RISE OF THE ORDER
GARRO: END TIMES
GARRO: SHORT STORIES
GARRO: COLLECTION
GARRO: HERESY
GARRO: FAITHLESS
GARRO: DESTROYER OF WORLDS
GARRO: COLLECTIONS BOOK 4-6
GARRO: MISTRESS OF BLOOD
GARRO: BEACON OF HOPE
GARRO: END OF DAYS

Winter Series- Fantasy Trilogy Books
WINTER'S COMING
WINTER'S HUNT
WINTER'S REVENGE
WINTER'S DISSENSION

Miscellaneous:
RETURN
FREEDOM
SALVATION
Reflection of Mount Flame
The Masked One
The Great Deer

Gay Romance Novellas
Breaking, Nursing, Repairing A Broken Heart
Jacob And Daniel
Fallen For A Lie
His Heartstopper
Spying And Weddings

All books in 'An Introductory Series':
Careers In Psychology
Psychology of Suicide
Dementia Psychology
Forensic Psychology of Terrorism And Hostage-Taking
Forensic Psychology of False Allegations
Year In Psychology
BIOLOGICAL PSYCHOLOGY 3RD EDITION
COGNITIVE PSYCHOLOGY THIRD EDITION
SOCIAL PSYCHOLOGY- 3RD EDITION
ABNORMAL PSYCHOLOGY 3RD EDITION
PSYCHOLOGY OF RELATIONSHIPS- 3RD EDITION
DEVELOPMENTAL PSYCHOLOGY 3RD EDITION
HEALTH PSYCHOLOGY
RESEARCH IN PSYCHOLOGY
A GUIDE TO MENTAL HEALTH AND TREATMENT AROUND THE WORLD- A GLOBAL LOOK AT DEPRESSION
FORENSIC PSYCHOLOGY
THE FORENSIC PSYCHOLOGY OF THEFT, BURGLARY AND OTHER CRIMES AGAINST PROPERTY
CRIMINAL PROFILING: A FORENSIC PSYCHOLOGY GUIDE TO FBI PROFILING AND GEOGRAPHICAL AND STATISTICAL PROFILING.
CLINICAL PSYCHOLOGY

GAY UNIVERSITY ROMANCE SHORT STORY COLLECTION

FORMULATION IN PSYCHOTHERAPY
PERSONALITY PSYCHOLOGY AND INDIVIDUAL DIFFERENCES
CLINICAL PSYCHOLOGY REFLECTIONS VOLUME 1
CLINICAL PSYCHOLOGY REFLECTIONS VOLUME 2
Clinical Psychology Reflections Volume 3
CULT PSYCHOLOGY
Police Psychology

A Psychology Student's Guide To University
How Does University Work?
A Student's Guide To University And Learning
University Mental Health and Mindset

Companion guides:
BIOLOGICAL PSYCHOLOGY 2ND EDITION WORKBOOK
COGNITIVE PSYCHOLOGY 2ND EDITION WORKBOOK
SOCIOCULTURAL PSYCHOLOGY 2ND EDITION WORKBOOK
ABNORMAL PSYCHOLOGY 2ND EDITION WORKBOOK
PSYCHOLOGY OF HUMAN RELATIONSHIPS 2ND EDITION WORKBOOK
HEALTH PSYCHOLOGY WORKBOOK
FORENSIC PSYCHOLOGY WORKBOOK

www.ingramcontent.com/pod-product-compliance
Lightning Source LLC
LaVergne TN
LVHW011848060526
838200LV00054B/4229